Magic
Animal Friends

For Isabella Banks

Special thanks to Valerie Wilding

ORCHARD BOOKS

First published in Great Britain in 2016 by The Watts Publishing Group

1 3 5 7 9 10 8 6 4 2

A CIP catalogue record for this book is available from the British Library.

ISBN 978 1 40834 104 9

Printed in Great Britain

The paper and board used in this book are made from wood from responsible sources

Orchard Books
An imprint of Hachette Children's Group
Part of The Watts Publishing Group Limited
Carmelite House, 50 Victoria Embankment, London EC4Y 0DZ

An Hachette UK Company
www.hachette.co.uk
www.hachettechildrens.co.uk

Hannah Honeypaw's Forgetful Day

Daisy Meadows

Sunshine Meadow

Hone
Tree

Goldie's Grotto

Toadstool Cafe

Toadstool Glade

Mr Cleverfeather's Inventing Shed

Mrs Taptree's Library

Friendship Tree

Parasol Tree

Grizelda
Worksho

Spa
Fa

Rushing Rapids

Butterfly Bowery

Entrance to the Caverns

Heart Trees

Nibblesqueak Bakery

Map of Friendship Forest
Woollyhop Shop
Harmony Hall Theatre
Petal Hill
Garland Green
Cherry Tree Corner
Treasure Tree
Bluebell Brook
Agatha Glitterwing's Shop
Slipperslide's Home
Sparklepaw Cottage
Coral Cove
Summer Sands Beach
Grizelda's Tower
Witchy Waste

Can you keep a secret? I thought you could!

Then I'll tell you about an enchanted wood.

It lies through the door in the old oak tree,

Let's go there now - just follow me!

We'll find adventure that never ends,

And meet the Magic Animal Friends!

Love,

Goldie the Cat

Contents

CHAPTER ONE: A New Furry Friend 9

CHAPTER TWO: A Heart-Shaped Path 21

CHAPTER THREE: Witches! 31

CHAPTER FOUR: Great-Uncle Greybear 43

CHAPTER FIVE: Busy Bees 57

CHAPTER SIX: Honeybuns 69

CHAPTER SEVEN: Trouble at Sparkly Falls 81

CHAPTER EIGHT: The Memory Tree 93

CHAPTER ONE

A New Furry Friend

Lily Hart was leaning over the fence of a rabbit run. As she dropped carrot sticks into a bowl, a little brown bunny with a bandaged ear looked up from the grass he was nibbling. He hopped over and began to crunch the carrots.

"You look so much better!" Lily said.

She stroked his soft fur and he wriggled his nose happily.

Lily's parents ran Helping Paw Wildlife Hospital in a large barn in their garden. It was surrounded by pens where poorly bunnies, foxes, hedgehogs and other animals stayed until they were better.

The gate rattled, and Lily turned to see Jess Forester coming over from the cottage where she lived with her dad. Jess was her best friend, and loved animals just as much as Lily did! The two girls helped care for the animals at the hospital as often as they could.

"Look what I've got!" said Jess. She showed Lily a brightly coloured box covered with drawings of animals.

"You've decorated our memory box!" Lily said. "It looks so beautiful!"

"That's not all," Jess said. "See what is inside!"

Lily opened it and gasped in surprise. "These are things from Friendship Forest!"

Friendship Forest was the girls' special secret. It was a hidden world where something amazing happened – all the animals could talk! Their friend Goldie the cat lived there, and whenever she came to find Jess and Lily, she took them on exciting adventures in the magical forest.

Lily touched a scrap of golden wool. "That's from the Woollyhops' shop," she said. "And here's a feather from Mr Cleverfeather the owl, and the bookmark Mrs Taptree the woodpecker gave us from her library." She smiled. "Jess, it's fantastic! It will remind us of our forest friends!"

"Our adventures there are so amazing, we could never forget them!" Jess laughed. "But we can look in the box whenever we miss Goldie and the other animals."

Lily nodded, smiling. "I wonder when we'll see her ag—" She stopped. "What's that?"

Jess listened.

"Mee-eww."

Lily spun round. A beautiful golden cat was rolling in a sunny spot. Her eyes were as green as spring grass.

"Goldie!" they cried, bending to stroke her shiny fur. The cat rubbed around their legs then darted off towards Brightley Stream.

Lily's eyes sparkled. "Goldie's taking us back to Friendship Forest! I wonder what memories we'll make this time?"

Goldie led the girls over the stream and into Brightley Meadow. Then they

ran towards a bare old tree.

The Friendship Tree!

As Goldie reached it, bunches of pink and white blossom appeared. Suddenly bees buzzed and tiny bluebirds chattered among the blooms.

Lily touched the words carved into the tree's bark, and the girls read them aloud. "Friendship Forest!"

They shivered with excitement as a door magically appeared in the trunk.

Goldie jumped through the doorway, and the girls ducked after her into the golden glow which made them tingle.

Jess and Lily knew that meant they were shrinking, just a little.

When the glow faded, the girls found themselves in bright sunshine, surrounded by tall leafy trees. The warm air was filled with the scent of orange daisies and lemon berries. A silver-speckled butterfly fluttered past, singing to herself.

"Welcome back to Friendship Forest," said a soft voice.

The girls turned. There was Goldie, standing upright, her golden scarf around her shoulders.

"It's so lovely to be here!" said Jess.

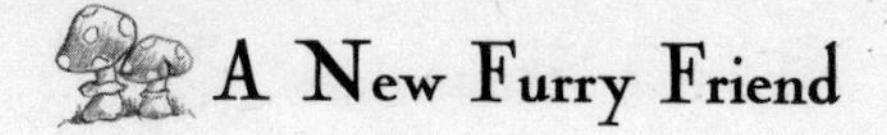

As the girls hugged their friend, Lily spotted a movement behind a bush. "Goldie, who's there?" she whispered.

"Someone wants to meet you," said the cat. "Come out, Hannah!"

A furry brown face, with big dark eyes, peeped from behind the bush. It was a little bear cub!

"Hello, Hannah!" said Jess.

Hannah ran to the girls. Her fluffy brown fur was the colour of delicious dark chocolate, and it glowed in the sunlight. She had a pretty pink scarf around her neck.

"Hello, I'm Hannah Honeypaw!"

she said. "Here's my best bear hug!"

She flung her arms around first Jess, then Lily, then Goldie.

"It's lovely to meet you," Lily said.

"You look very excited!" said Jess.

Goldie smiled. "Today is Hannah's favourite day of the year."

"It's Honey Harvest Day!" said the little bear, bouncing up and down. "The bees bring their honey to Toadstool Glade, and everyone tastes it. Then we choose the yummiest honey and get to take some home for later! Would you like to come?"

"We'd love to!" said Lily. "It's so *sweet* of you to ask us."

Hannah giggled, then licked her lips. "Yummy honey – I can't wait!"

Jess grinned, thinking of the memory box they had left back at Helping Paw. She hoped they were about to have another unforgettable adventure!

CHAPTER TWO

A Heart-Shaped Path

Jess and Lily both held one of Hannah's soft paws as they followed Goldie towards Toadstool Glade.

All their animal friends waved as they passed. "Hello, girls!" a mole in purple glasses called as she popped her head out of the ground.

"It's Lola Velvetnose!" cried Jess and Lily. "Hi, Lola!"

The door of a tiny house tucked into the crook of a mossy root swung open and a group of snails crept out.

"It's the Curlyshell family!" Lily said, giving them a wave.

"They're probably off to the Honey Harvest too…" Hannah's voice trailed away, and she stopped for a moment, looking puzzled.

"What's wrong?" Lily asked.

Hannah scratched her head. "I think I've forgotten something."

"What sort of thing?" asked Jess.

Hannah's little button nose twitched and she frowned. "I can't remember," she said, "but I'm sure it's very important."

"Don't worry," said Goldie. "I know what will help you remember. The Memory Tree! We've enough time to get there and back before the Honey Harvest starts."

"Oh, yes!" cried Hannah, clapping her paws. "Let's go!"

"What's the Memory Tree?" Lily asked, as they hurried down a narrow track.

"It's one of four trees called the Heart

Trees," Goldie explained as she led the way. "Any animal can go to them when they need help. The Memory Tree helps you remember things, the Laughter Tree makes you happy, the Sweet Dreams Tree gives you a good night's sleep, and the Kindness Tree helps all the animals look after each other."

As they turned onto a soft mossy path, Jess gave a cry. The path was lined with pink flowers with deep green leaves.

"Look!" said Jess. "All the leaves are heart-shaped!"

Goldie smiled. "The path is heart-shaped, too," she said. "It leads all around the Heart Trees."

Lily smiled at Jess. "Friendship Forest seems more magical every time we come here!" she said.

They hurried along the beautiful path until Goldie stopped in front of a huge tree with a broad trunk. Its wide branches curved gently up towards the sun. Its leaves were shaped like keys, and clusters of delicate yellow flowers hung from every branch.

"Here we are," Goldie said.

The girls gazed at it in wonder.

"It's so pretty!" said Lily.

Goldie smiled. "This is the Memory Tree. It helps to unlock memories."

"Oh! That's why the leaves are key-shaped!" said Jess.

"That's right," said Goldie.

She pointed her paw towards a large hollow at the very bottom of the trunk.

Hannah and the girls crouched down to see a glass heart nestled inside, glistening like a beautiful diamond.

Lily gasped. "What is it?"

"That heart holds the tree's magic," said Goldie. "If you want to remember something, you pick a flower, ask a question, and look at the heart for the answer." She grinned. "If you don't ask anything, the heart will show your favourite memory. Let's try it!"

Jess, Lily and Goldie each picked a yellow flower, then Jess lifted Hannah up so she could pick one, too.

Lily gazed at the heart. "I can only see the heart," she said, confused.

"Keep looking," said Goldie, staring at the glass. "I can see my favourite memory – me picnicking at Sparkly Falls!"

Hannah gave a shout. "Mine is me eating my favourite honey!"

Everyone giggled. Then Lily gasped as the glass heart suddenly shimmered, and a picture appeared of a very tall tree covered in fruit and nuts. "Wow!" she cried.

"Mine's when I saw the Treasure Tree for the first time!"

"Mine, too!" said Jess. "We've got the same favourite memory – no wonder we're best friends!"

They all laughed. Then Hannah reached up her paws.

"Could you lift me up again, Jess?" she asked. "Then I can ask the tree what I've forgotten."

Jess picked up the little bear. Hannah reached out to take another flower, but just then a yellow-green orb of light came floating straight towards them!

 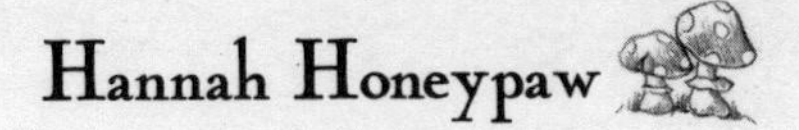

"Look out!" Lily cried.

Jess hugged Hannah protectively. "Oh, no!" she said. "It's Grizelda!"

Grizelda was a bad witch who wanted to get rid of the animals so she could have Friendship Forest all to herself. So far, Jess, Lily and Goldie had always managed to stop her horrible plans.

"What's she up to?" Jess whispered.

"I don't know," Lily said nervously, "but whatever nasty plan she's come up with, she's got help!"

There wasn't just one orb of light – there were five!

CHAPTER THREE

Witches!

The girls stared in horror as the lights flew into the clearing.

Behind Grizelda's yellow-green orb bobbed four others – one purple, one blue, one green and one yellow. The biggest orb burst into a shower of smelly sparks. In its place stood Grizelda the witch!

Grizelda was wearing a purple tunic, black trousers and high-heeled boots. Her green hair swirled wildly around her head, like squabbling snakes.

"Ha! It's the interfering girls and their cat," she sneered. "And a silly bear!"

Hannah shrank back behind the girls nervously.

"Leave her alone, Grizelda!" shouted Jess. "She's only little."

"I've got some little friends, too," Grizelda said, and snapped her fingers.

The four smaller orbs burst into showers of sparks: purple, blue, green and yellow.

In their places stood four small witches, about the same age as the girls.

"Oh, no," Lily groaned. "I hope they aren't horrible troublemakers like Grizelda!"

Grizelda laughed. "Of course they are! They're staying in my tower, learning powerful magic."

"Bad magic, I bet!" said Jess.

Grizelda screeched with laughter. "Of course! Witches! Show these pests what you can do!"

A witch with scruffy purple hair stepped forward. "I'm Thistle," she said.

"I'm the best at flying!"

She climbed on her broomstick, and flew in a wobbly circle. As she landed, Thistle nearly crashed.

"Oopsy woopsy!" she said, standing up and shaking her messy purple hair out of her eyes.

"Thistle's not as good at flying as she thinks she is!" whispered Lily.

The second witch had long, twisty hair and carried a large blue spider. He was busy spinning a web, humming as he worked.

"I'm Ivy," said the witch. "And this is Sidney the spider. He's made a yucky web for you to get stuck in!"

She grabbed Sidney's web and flung it at the girls. Luckily, it went too high and stuck on a branch above their heads.

The third witch had a big puffball of yellow hair. "I'm Dandelion," she said. "I'm best at potions!" She took a bottle from her pocket. "Watch me turn those pebbles into toads!"

Dandelion sprinkled her potion over some smooth grey stones. With a flash, the pebbles turned into biscuits!

Thistle dived for the biscuits and took a bite. "Ugh!

You silly thing, Dandelion. Your biscuits are made of stone and they taste like burnt toads!"

Suddenly, they heard a loud rustling in a bush behind them. They turned to see a fourth witch leap out.

"Boo!" the witch cried, then scowled. "I'm Nettle. Made you jump, didn't I?"

Lily and Jess couldn't help laughing. "These witches aren't very good at magic!" Jess whispered.

Grizelda glared at her. "My students are magical enough to stop *you*. And so am I!"

Grizelda pointed a bony finger. A bolt of yellow light shot out, heading straight towards the hollow in the trunk of the Memory Tree.

"No!" cried Goldie.

They watched in horror as the gorgeous glass heart floated out. It trembled in the air for a moment before splitting into three pieces. Grizelda snapped her fingers, and the three pieces vanished.

Jess and Lily gasped.

Hannah pointed a trembling paw at the tree, crying out, "Look at the flowers!"

The yellow blooms were drooping, and the key-shaped leaves were falling to the ground.

Grizelda was delighted. "The tree's heart is broken!" she cackled. "Broken into three heart pieces! Ha! Without the Memory Tree's magic, all the animals will become forgetful. Soon they won't even remember where they live. They'll wander away, and I'll have Friendship Forest all to myself. Haa!"

Hannah hid behind Goldie, but the girls stood their ground.

"We'll find a way to stop your horrid spell!" shouted Lily.

"You won't," Grizelda sneered. Then she pointed to Thistle. "You stay here and make sure no one interferes with my spell!"

Thistle nodded eagerly, and Grizelda snapped her fingers and vanished in a shower of stinking sparks.

Ivy, Nettle and Dandelion copied her, snapping their fingers and disappearing in bursts of colourful sparkles. Thistle grinned wickedly at the girls. Then she snapped her fingers and transformed into a purple orb, which zoomed forwards, accidentally knocking into a tree before disappearing into the forest.

The girls were too dismayed to speak.

Hannah Honeypaw looked up at them, her big dark eyes swimming with tears.

"How can we save the Memory Tree?" she asked.

"I don't know," said Jess.

Lily hugged the bear. "But we promise, Hannah – we'll break the spell. Somehow…"

CHAPTER FOUR

Great-Uncle Greybear

The girls, Goldie and Hannah looked sadly up at the Memory Tree. Its flowers had wilted and its leaves had begun to drop as though it were autumn. Tears were dropping down from Hannah's cheeks, too.

The flower Hannah had picked earlier

was still in her paws, its petals still bright yellow. Jess reached for it gently and tucked it behind one of Hannah's soft, brown ears. "There, there," she said. "We'll bring back the other flowers, too."

Hannah wiped her eyes and gave a little grin.

Lily frowned thoughtfully. "Goldie," she said. "Has the Memory Tree ever lost its heart before?"

"I don't know," said Goldie sadly. "I don't know very much about the Heart Trees."

Hannah thought for a moment.

Then her eyes lit up. "My Great-Uncle Greybear is always telling me stories about the Heart Trees!" she cried. "They were planted when he was a cub. Perhaps he can help."

"That's a brilliant idea!" said Jess.

Hannah jumped up and down with excitement. "Great-Uncle Greybear's den is this way," she said. "Come on!"

Hannah led the friends along a stony path lined with starflower bushes.

"Look!" Lily pointed. In a clearing was a tall stork. He was staring up at a colourful patchwork hot-air balloon and scratching his head with a wingtip.

"It's Captain Ace!" Jess cried.

"What's wrong, Captain?" Goldie called.

The stork turned. "I'm wondering what that big floaty thing is," he said.

"It's your balloon!" explained Jess. "You use it to fly all your friends around the forest."

"Oh," said Captain Ace. He scratched his head again. "I must have forgotten."

Goldie pointed across the

clearing to
where some
tiny mice were
scurrying along,
peering all around them. "It's
the Twinkletails," she said.
"They look puzzled too."

Lily called to the biggest mouse.
"Molly! Are you OK?"

"We can't remember
the way home," Molly
squeaked.

"Follow that path." Lily pointed. "And
turn right at Crystal Pond."

"Thank you!" said Molly, and the Twinkletails scurried away.

"Oh, dear," Goldie said. "Everybody must be forgetting things because the Memory Tree has lost its magic."

"Then let's hurry before it gets any worse," said Lily.

"It's strange," said Jess. "The animals are forgetting things, but we're not."

Lily thought for a moment. "We're from the human world, and Goldie was once a stray there, so perhaps that's why we're all OK," she said.

Goldie nodded. "And look!" she said,

pointing to the flower behind Hannah's ear. "Hannah's still got a flower from the Memory Tree. I bet it's protecting her from the spell!"

Jess and Lily glanced at each other. Hannah's flower hadn't wilted like the ones on the Memory Tree, but its petals were already drooping. After it wilted, would Hannah forget everything too?

They hurried on through the forest. Finally Hannah cried, "We're here! This is Great-Uncle Greybear's den."

The girls looked around, but all they could see was a tree trunk covered in ivy.

"Where?" asked Lily.

Hannah ran to the tree and knocked on the trunk. *Knock, knock, knock.*

"It's me, Uncle," Hannah called, knocking again. "And my friends Goldie, Jess and Lily."

"Hannah!" said a deep, gruffly voice. "Come right in, dear!"

A patch of moss by the trunk moved aside to reveal a staircase going down into the ground.

The girls grinned at each other, then they followed Hannah down the stairs into a cosy room with squishy armchairs,

a red rug and a crackling log fire. Flower paintings hung on the wooden walls, and in the middle of the room a big grey bear stood smiling, holding a broom.

He bowed. "Do sit down. I was just—I can't remember what I was doing!"

Jess pointed to his broom. "I think you might have been sweeping, Great-Uncle Greybear."

"Ah, yes!" said Great-Uncle Greybear, looking down at the broom. "That's it!"

"He's getting forgetful already," Lily whispered to Jess. "Let's ask him about Heart Trees, quickly."

"Great-Uncle Greybear," Jess said. "Can you tell us about the Heart Trees?"

"Heart Trees?" said the bear. "Never heard of them."

"They're the oldest trees in Friendship Forest," said Lily.

"Friendship Forest?" he said. "Never heard of that, either. Where's my, er...my sweepy thing?" he said.

"It's in your paw," said Jess, pointing to the broom.

"Ah, yes!" said Great-Uncle Greybear. Then he began sweeping the bookcase.

"He's forgotten everything!" Lily said.

Honey's eyes filled with tears again, and Jess looked at Lily in dismay.

Then Great-Uncle Greybear spoke. "Maybe my scrapbooks can help you young bears," he said. He stopped sweeping the bookcase and took down a pile of scrapbooks.

The friends took one each and began searching through them. The pages were filled with snippets of writing, pictures and pressed leaves.

"They're just like our memory box, Jess!" said Lily.

"Here's one from when Great-Uncle

Greybear was a cub," cried Goldie.

The others peered over her shoulder as she flicked past school reports, swimming certificates and pages of drawings.

"Go back!" cried Jess suddenly. "There's something about the Heart Trees."

Goldie turned the page and there was a whole spread full of doodles, scribbles and pictures – all about the Heart Trees!

Lily read the pages out loud:

"*After the trees were planted, the wisest animals protected the Memory Tree's heart. If someone harms the tree, its heart will split into three pieces, which must be found and put back together. Wherever the last three memories shown by the tree took place, that's where the heart pieces will be hidden!*"

"The last three memories the tree showed were ours!" said Lily.

Jess whirled Hannah around. "Now we know how to fix the Memory Tree!"

CHAPTER FIVE

Busy Bees

"Hannah," said Lily, glancing nervously at the bear's flower. "Can you remember your favourite memory? The one the tree showed you?"

The little brown bear bounced in excitement. "I can, I can!" she said. "I was helping the bees harvest Goodluck Honey, and they let me eat some, and—"

But just then, a petal dropped from Hannah's flower, and her face fell. "But I can't remember where."

Jess and Lily looked at each other in alarm.

"Don't worry," said Goldie. "We'll try Toadstool Glade. The bees will all be taking their honey there for the Honey Harvest. They can tell us where they get Goodluck Honey."

They thanked Great-Uncle Greybear and put his scrapbooks away.

Hannah gave him her best bear hug

and tugged the broom from his paw.

"Just stay here, Great-Uncle Greybear," she said. "Me and my friends will make everything right again."

He gave a gruffly chuckle. "Dear little bear," he said. "You're always looking after me!"

They all said goodbye, and the four friends headed for Toadstool Glade.

But when they got there, there wasn't a bee in sight. Instead, lots of animals were wandering around with puzzled looks on their faces.

"Where was I going?" asked Lucy

Longwhiskers the rabbit.

"Why am I carrying these hazelnuts?" wondered Mrs Flufftail the squirrel.

"What a lovely forest!" said Ellie Featherbill the duckling. "I wonder what it's called."

Jess was horrified. "They're forgetting everything!"

"And the bees must have forgotten where to go for the Honey Harvest," Goldie said anxiously. "They should be here by now!"

"Wait!"

cried Lily.

"I can hear buzzing!"

She ran into the trees, followed by Jess, Hannah and Goldie.

Moments later, they came across a swarm of fluffy gold and brown bees buzzing around in mid-air. The largest, fluffiest one wore a tiny golden crown.

"It's Queenie Busywing!" cried Jess. "Your Majesty? May we talk to you?"

The queen bee flew down to Jess's outstretched hand. "*Bzzzzzzz*. Do I know you?" she asked. "Never mind.

We are puzzled. We have forgotten what we are supposed to be doing."

"It's Honey Harvest Day," said Lily.

"You're right," said Queenie. "But where is the honey? We must have left it somewhere..."

"We need to find the honey, too," Jess told her friends. "The heart piece could be with it."

Hannah sniffed, her little brown nose woffling from side to side. She sniffed again. "I smell honey!"

"Hooray!" cried Goldie. "Can you lead us to it, Hannah?"

"Yes!" said Hannah. "This way."

Off she ran, followed by Jess, Lily, Goldie and a swarm of bees. They darted through the trees until Hannah stopped in a clearing full of clover.

"The honey smell's really strong now," said Hannah, sniffing. "It must be here somewhere."

As Lily looked around, something caught her eye. Half-hidden by tree branches was a wooden wagon, piled with honey pots!

The bees buzzed happily around the wagon. "Thank you," said Queenie. "You've found our missing honey!"

"Queenie," said Jess. "Can you tell us where the Goodluck Honey is harvested?"

"But of course!" said the bee. "Just look around – you're in Clover Clearing! Four-leaf clovers are perfect for Goodluck Honey!"

Hannah jumped up and down, clapping her paws together. "This is it!" she cried. "This is where I ate it! The memory I saw was here!"

"You're right," said Jess, pointing to

a corner of the clearing. On top of the honeypots was a piece of glass, giving off a magical glow.

Lily gasped. "It's one of the heart pieces!" She reached to grab it.

But, suddenly, something swooped low over her head, and she tripped. She glanced up as she fell and saw Thistle on her broomstick.

"Oh, no!" Lily cried.

The others ran to help her up as Thistle swooped down, scattering the bees. "You're not getting that heart piece back!" yelled Thistle.

The little witch leaned off her broomstick to grab it. But the broomstick wobbled and she missed, grabbing a honeypot instead.

Jess reached for the heart piece but, before she could reach it, Thistle flew over again. She flicked the lid off the honeypot and tipped the honey out. It splattered to the ground, just missing Jess, Lily, Goldie and Hannah as they jumped out of the way.

"Ha!" cackled Thistle. But her broomstick wobbled again and she thumped into the side of the honey wagon. "Oopsy woopsy!" she cried. The pot flew into the air, tipping the rest of the honey over her purple hair.

"Uh-oh!" said Lily. "If she's anything like Grizelda, she's going to get really cross now!"

But Thistle licked her lips as the honey trickled over her face. "Mmm! Yummy!" she said with a grin. She scooped honey from her hair and licked her fingers.

"Quick!" said Goldie. "Let's get the

heart piece while she's busy eating!"

Lily snatched it from the top of the wagon. "Got it!"

"We'll keep her busy with more honey," said Queenie, as the bees flew another pot over to Thistle.

"Thank you!" the four friends cried, and rushed into the trees before Thistle could see where they were going. They stopped to catch their breath, grinning at each other.

"Hooray!" cried Hannah. "We've found the first heart piece!"

CHAPTER SIX

Honeybuns

The four friends crept through the forest, with Lily holding tightly to the heart piece. When they were sure that Thistle wasn't following them, they stopped.

"Girls, your memory took place at the Treasure Tree," said Goldie, "so that's where the second piece will be."

"We'd better hurry, before Thistle realises what's happened," said Jess.

They set off down the well-worn path towards the Treasure Tree. Soon they reached the clearing where the huge tree stood. Its thick, leafy branches spread so wide and high it seemed to fill the sky. Fruits and nuts of every sort hung from its branches, ready for the forest animals to help themselves. On the ground by the trunk were three baskets.

Hannah peeked into one of them. "Mmm, iced honeybuns! They must be for the Honey Harvest!"

"They're probably from the Nibblesqueak Bakery," said Lily. "But why are they here?"

"I know!" Jess said. "Look who's sitting on the lowest branch!"

Lily peered through the leaves and saw three hamsters, looking very upset.

"It's Jenny, Penny and Olivia Nibblesqueak!" she cried. "Whatever's wrong?"

"We're stuck!" said Olivia, her whiskers quivering. "We were collecting raspberries to decorate our honeybuns, but we've forgotten how to get down!"

"We might fall!" wailed Jenny.

"Help!" squeaked Penny.

"Don't worry," said Lily.

She, Jess and Goldie each lifted down a trembling hamster and set them carefully on the ground, while Hannah clambered up the knobbly tree trunk to get their basket of raspberries.

"Thank you!" squeaked all the hamsters gratefully.

"The heart piece must be up the Treasure Tree somewhere," said Goldie to the girls and Hannah. "We've got to climb up and find it." She turned to the Nibblesqueaks. "If you see a witch, will you shout to let us know?"

"We will!" cried the hamsters. The four friends started to climb the Treasure Tree. They used vines to scramble up, past golden pineapples and spotted melons, fuzzy coconuts and tiger-striped tangerines. Instead of using the vines, Hannah scrambled up the tree trunk.

"Wow!" said Lily. "Your legs may be little, Hannah, but they're strong!"

Higher and higher they went. As the

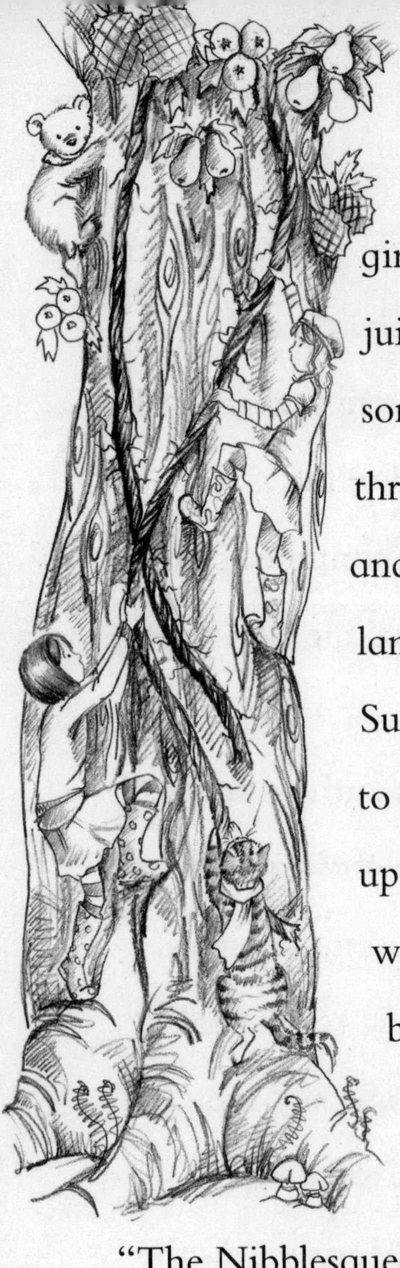

girls passed bunches of juicy red sunberries, something swished through the branches – and a ripe, squishy plum landed on Jess's shoulder. Suddenly, the tree began to shake, and Jess looked up to see a broomstick wobbling through the branches.

"It's Thistle – she's found us!" cried Jess. "The Nibblesqueaks must have forgotten to warn us!" Lily sighed.

"Hee hee!" Thistle giggled, as she swooped unsteadily towards them, flinging more plums. Hannah wiped away a squashed plum from her paw.

"We can't climb while she's doing that," Goldie said crossly.

Lily ducked as a plum whizzed past. "Remember how much Thistle liked the honey? And how she tried to eat Dandelion's biscuits?" she said. "Maybe she'd like honeybuns, too. They might make her leave us alone for long enough to find the heart piece!"

Lily clambered as quickly as she could back down the tree. "Nibblesqueaks," she cried, "could I have some honeybuns, please? We need to stop that witch!"

The hamsters handed some honeybuns to Lily and she waved them in the air. "Ooh, Thistle!" she yelled at the witch, who was whizzing around the tree. "Look at these delicious honeybuns!"

Thistle zoomed down, tumbling head-over-heels to the ground. "Oopsy woopsy!" she said. She took a honeybun and stuffed it in her mouth. "Mmmmmm," she said happily, as she chewed.

"Have another one," said Lily. Above, she could see Jess, Goldie and Hannah climbing higher up the Treasure Tree.

Jess grinned as she looked down and saw Thistle snatch another honeybun from Lily. The plan had worked! And as she started climbing again, she spotted the heart piece, resting on a broad branch, and glowing gently. "There!" she cried. "But it's too high up for me."

"I can't climb that far, either," said Goldie, shaking her head.

"I can!" said Hannah, and she was off, climbing paw over paw. In moments, she stretched out and grabbed the heart piece.

"Well done, Hannah!" cried Jess.

The three friends carefully made their way down the tree. On the ground, Thistle was gobbling her way through a heap of honeybuns. She had cake crumbs

and icing all around her mouth.

"Come on," said Goldie. "Maybe the honeybuns will keep her busy for longer than the honey did!"

"Thank you for helping us," Lily said to the hamsters. "We'd have been stuck without your honeybuns."

"Thank you for rescuing us too!" said Olivia Nibblesqueak. "Goodbye!"

The four friends waved goodbye and hurried back among the trees.

"There's only one more heart piece to find!" said Jess, happily. "We've almost done it!"

"My memory was at Sparkly Falls, so that's where the final heart piece will be!" said Goldie.

But Hannah suddenly stopped and scratched her head. "What heart piece?" she asked. "What's Sparkly Falls?"

The others stared in shock.

"The flower behind Hannah's ear," Jess cried, as more yellow petals floated to the ground. "It's wilting!"

Goldie nodded, her tail twitching with worry. "Come on, straight to Sparkly Falls," she said. "And hurry!"

CHAPTER SEVEN

Trouble at Sparkly Falls

Lily, Jess and Goldie raced through the trees, with Hannah riding on Jess's back. As they darted down the path to Sparkly Falls, they saw an old owl ahead. He had a wooden cart loaded with bits and pieces of machinery and a long fishing rod.

"It's Mr Cleverfeather!" said Jess.

"Mood gorning," the owl said when they reached him, mixing up his words as always. "I mean, good morning. My name's Mr Cleverfeather. Mice to neat you. Er, nice to meet you."

"He's forgotten who we are," whispered Lily. Aloud, she said, "Hello, Mr Cleverfeather! What are you doing?"

Mr Cleverfeather looked at his cart and

scratched his head. "I'm trying to work out what these things are."

"Oh, no!" said Lily. "He's forgotten about his inventions." She put an arm around the worried owl. "Don't worry, Mr Cleverfeather. We—"

There was a sudden crashing noise in the treetops, and Thistle swooped into view on her broomstick. She bashed a branch and smashed into a berry bush.

"Oopsy!" she cried.

She bounced across the top of a prickly holly tree.

"Woopsy!" she shrieked.

"Quick!" Goldie cried. "We have to get to Sparkly Falls before Thistle does!"

"You'll remember your inventions soon, we promise!" Lily called over her shoulder to Mr Cleverfeather, as they ran down the path. There, in front of them, was Sparkly Falls. The waterfall tumbled wildly over a cliff, foaming over the rocks below.

Jess gave a cry. "Look! The heart piece! It's on that rock, near the waterfall."

"Oh, no!" said Lily. "We'll never reach it. And the water is moving really fast. It's too dangerous for swimming."

But Jess had an idea. "Mr Cleverfeather's fishing rod!" she said. "If it's one of his inventions then it won't be an ordinary fishing rod – I bet it'll do something magical. Let's borrow it!"

As she and Goldie sprinted back the way they had come, Lily and Hannah kept a lookout for Thistle.

"Hurry, Jess and Goldie," Lily murmured.

Hannah gave a shout and pointed her paw in the air. Thistle was flying on her broomstick over the trees towards Sparkly Falls! She had leaves and twigs stuck in her purple hair, and icing all around her mouth. "Ha ha!" she called down to Lily as she flew overhead. "The final heart piece! I'm going to get it!"

Lily groaned. "We should have brought some honeybuns to distract her! Oh, what are we going to do?"

Thistle swooped down to Sparkly Falls. She leaned over, grabbing for the heart piece, but missed. She zigzagged back

towards the bank, then toppled off her broomstick, landing on the soft grass near Lily and Hannah.

"Look!" said Lily, pointing to Thistle's broomstick, which kept on flying straight into the forest. "You'd better catch it!" Lily told the clumsy witch. Thistle scrambled to her feet and ran after it.

"Phew!" Lily cried.

"Oh, no!" Hannah tugged Lily's sleeve. "Who are *they*?"

Lily turned anxiously, then smiled as she saw Jess, Goldie and Mr Cleverfeather hurrying out of the trees. Jess was carrying the fishing rod.

"Hurry!" cried Lily. "Thistle's here!"

Jess sprinted to the water's edge with the rod. She drew it back, then brought it forward over her shoulder. The green fishing line soared far out into the water, but dropped short of the heart piece.

Jess groaned. "It doesn't reach!"

"Let me try," said Hannah.

She took the rod from Jess, then clambered over the rocks at the edge of

the churning water, making her way closer to the heart piece.

"Careful!" called Goldie.

Hannah's paws gripped the rocks safely. But, suddenly, she stopped. "Why did I come out here?" she asked. Then she pointed to the bottom of the fishing rod. "And what's this button for?"

Lily and Jess looked at each other, and then back to the fishing rod. "I didn't notice a button!" said Jess.

"I bet that's how you make it work," said Lily. "Push it, Hannah!"

Hannah pushed the button. The line

magically wound around the heart piece and tied itself into a bow.

"Hooray!" cheered Goldie and the girls. Mr Cleverfeather gave a happy hoot.

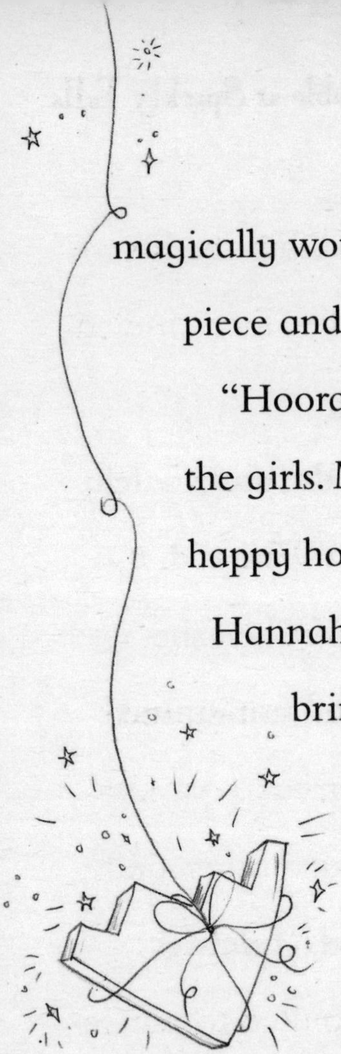

Hannah reeled the line in, bringing the heart piece with it. She climbed back onto the shore and the friends pulled her into a hug.

"A bear hug for a brilliant bear!" Lily said. "But I wonder what happened to Thistle?"

They turned around and saw the little witch sitting under a tree, her face cradled in her hands.

"Oh, no," said Lily. "She's crying!"

They hurried over to her. "What is it, Thistle?" asked Goldie gently.

The witch looked up. Her tear-stained face was sticky with honey, cake crumbs and icing.

"My broomstick ran into a tree! It's broken!" she wailed. She pointed to where it lay on the grass, snapped in half.

"Poor Thistle," Jess whispered.

"Who's Thistle?" asked Hannah,

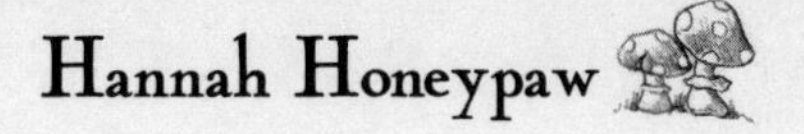

scratching her furry head.

"Hannah's forgetting everything!" said Lily. "We need to get the heart pieces back to the Memory Tree."

Mr Cleverfeather gave a hoot. "Don't worry, wittle itch," he said. "I can fix your broomstick." He frowned. "If I can remember how to mend things."

"Thanks, Mr Cleverfeather!" said Goldie. "Now let's go back to the Memory Tree – as fast as we can!"

CHAPTER EIGHT

The Memory Tree

They ran through the forest until at last they arrived back at the Memory Tree. It was completely bare and lifeless. All its leaves and flowers lay in dried, brown piles around its trunk.

"Let's hope this works!" said Lily.

She knelt and placed the first heart

piece in the hollow. Jess put in the second.

"Hannah," said Goldie. "We couldn't have done this without you. You should put in the third piece."

"What's this?" asked Hannah, looking down at the piece she held in her paws.

"We're trying to bring the tree back to life, remember?" Lily said gently.

The little bear looked puzzled, but placed the third heart piece between the other two.

The hollow filled with sparkles and the girls held their breath.

The sparkles faded as the three heart pieces joined into one glass heart!

The Memory Tree's branches rustled as key-shaped leaves sprang from them and yellow flowers burst into bloom.

The girls looked at Hannah, whose eyes suddenly widened. "The Memory Tree!" she cried. "I remember!"

"We've done it!" Lily cried, clasping Hannah's paws. Jess held Goldie's and they danced around.

There was a cheer from behind. "Wow-de-wowowow!"

Thistle landed gracefully behind them. Her broomstick was back in one piece, its wood shining and its bristles neatly groomed.

"Thistle!" Jess cried in alarm. "Leave the Memory Tree alone!"

"I will," the small witch said, smiling. "I'm sorry I tried to stop you fixing it. I… I like Friendship Forest. Everyone's kind –

and the food is yummy!"

"Do you mean it?" Lily asked in surprise.

"Yes," said the witch. "Even though I wasn't very nice, the bees shared their honey, the hamsters gave me cakes, and Mr Cleverfeather fixed my broomstick." She pointed at it, grinning. "I'm a much better flyer now. Watch this!"

She lifted off and did a neat loop-the-loop, landing gently on her feet.

"That was great!" said Goldie.

"Perfect!" Jess said with a laugh.

Lily took Thistle's hand. "Now you

know how wonderful Friendship Forest is, do you promise you won't spoil it?"

"I promise!" said Thistle. "And instead of going back to Grizelda's tower to learn horrible magic, I'll stay here and guard the Memory Tree."

"That's brilliant!" said Jess, giving Thistle a hug.

"I bet the animals would help you build a lovely home nearby!" said Lily.

"We'd be happy to," said Goldie, smiling. "But for now, let's go to the Honey Harvest!"

As girls and Goldie turned to leave,

Hannah cried, "Wait!"

She scrambled up the tree trunk, picked a flower and jumped down.

"I must find out what I forgot this morning!" she explained. "That's why we came here in the first place."

The others clustered around as she peered into the glass heart.

"Of course!" Hannah said. "I forgot to bring my honey jar to the Honey Harvest! I'll need it to take some honey home. And I'll get jars for Lily and Jess, so they can have some, too!"

Toadstool Glade was crowded with tables piled high with honeypots. Everyone chatted and laughed as they tasted all the different honeys.

"Hello, dear bears," came a voice from behind them. Great-Uncle Greybear padded over, his paws full of jars.

"Thank you for bringing back my memory," he said, taking a spoonful of honey. "It would have been a shame to forget to come and taste this!"

Queenie Busywing flew over with her bees, each carrying a square of toast spread with honey for them to try.

"Delicious!" said Lily, nibbling a piece.

The little bear was by one of the tables, filling a jar with Goodluck Honey and getting sticky honey all over her fur.

"I can see why you're called Hannah Honeypaw!" Jess joked.

"I'll take some to Thistle later," Hannah told them.

"No need," said Goldie. "Look!"

The little witch stood at the edge of the glade. "Am I invited too?" she asked.

"Of course you are!" said Jess.

Hannah gave Thistle the honey jar and a big bear hug.

"Thanks, Hannah!" said Thistle. "You'll have to come to my new home and share it with me."

Jess smiled. "This has been so much fun! But now it's time for Lily and me to go home, too."

The girls hugged Thistle, then turned to Hannah, who threw herself at them.

"This is my biggest bear hug!" she said. Then she handed them their own jar of Goodluck Honey to take with them.

Goldie took Lily and Jess back to the Friendship Tree.

"You'll get us if Grizelda tries any more mean spells, won't you?" asked Lily.

"Of course." Goldie smiled and hugged them both. "Friendship Forest couldn't manage without you!"

She touched a paw to the tree, and a door appeared in the trunk.

"Bye, Goldie!" said Lily.

"See you soon!" called Jess, as they stepped into the shimmering glow. They felt the tingle that meant they were returning to their usual size. When the light faded, they were back home in Brightley Meadow.

"What a fantastic adventure!" said Jess, as they walked back to Helping Paw. She held up her jar. "And here's another lovely memory of Friendship Forest!"

Lily laughed. "That honey's too yummy to put in our memory box."

"You're right!" Jess grinned. "Let's make some toast – with lots of Goodluck Honey!"

The End

Tiny dormouse Freya Snufflenose is very excited about performing in the Funny Fair. But when Grizelda and her young witches attack the Laughter Tree, all the fun goes out of Friendship Forest! Can Lily, Jess and Freya bring the laughter back?

Find out in the next adventure,

Freya Snufflenose's Lost Laugh

Turn over for a sneak peek . . .

Jess nudged Lily. "Look at that adorable little dormouse doing acrobatics," she said.

The tiny golden-brown creature had soft round ears, delicate whiskers and a long fluffy tail. She finished with three roly-polys, then sprang to her feet. As everyone clapped, she picked up her blue purse and a large purple flower, which she tucked behind her ear.

Jess knelt beside her. "Hello!" she said. "I'm Jess, and this is my best friend, Lily."

The dormouse's big dark eyes sparkled. "I'm Freya Snufflenose!"

"I like your purple flower," said Jess.

Freya giggled. "Would you like to smell it?"

As Jess leaned over to sniff the flower, it puffed a cloud of glitter all over the dormouse's fur.

"Oh, no!" Freya cried. "My joke flower was supposed to puff all over Jess. Bother!"

Read

Freya Snufflenose's Lost Laugh

to find out what happens next!

Can Jess and Lily stop Grizelda and her young witches from ruining the Heart Trees? Read all the books in series four to find out!

COMING SOON!
Look out for
Jess and Lily's
next adventure:
Maisie Dappletrot
Saves the Day!

www.magicanimalfriends.com

Puzzle Fun!

Hannah Honeypaw, Lottie Littlestripe, Freya Snufflenose and Matilda Fluffywing are all mixed up! How many of each character can you count?

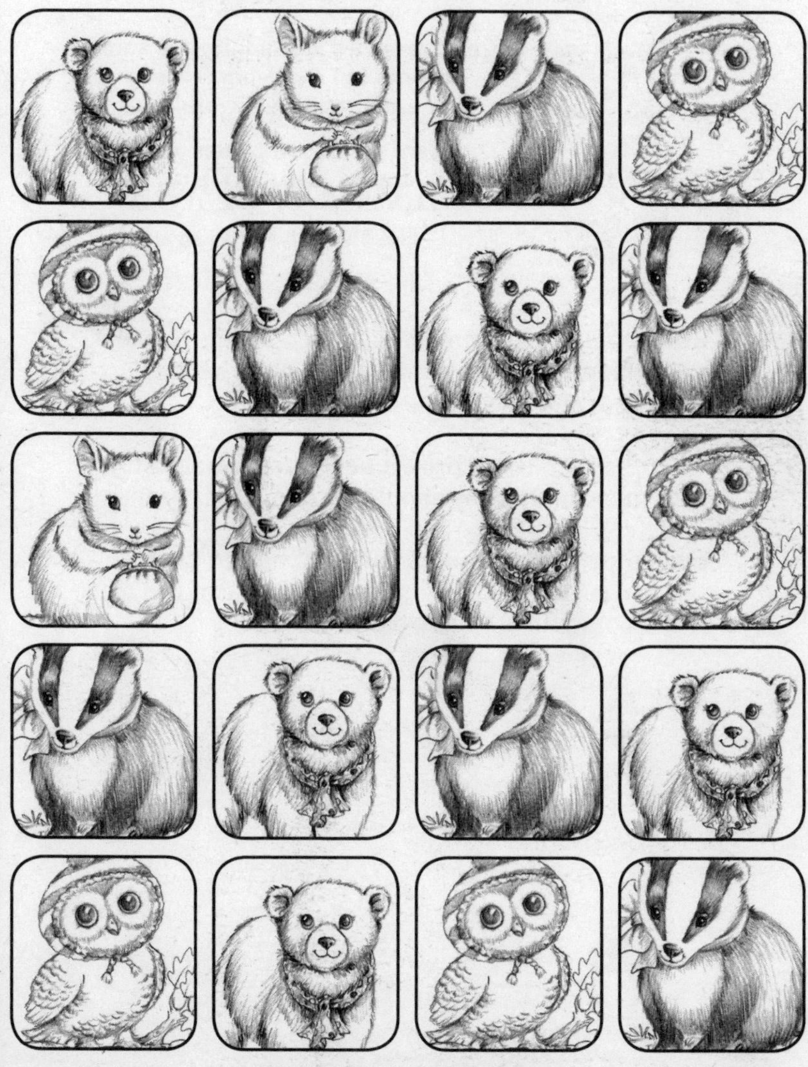

5 7 2 6

Jess and Lily's Animal Facts

Lily and Jess love lots of different animals – both in Friendship Forest and in the real world.

Here are their top facts about

BROWN BEARS

like Hannah Honeypaw:

- Brown bears are omnivores, which means they eat everything! They eat a mixture of nuts, berries, meat, fish and even honey.
- After they are born, brown bear cubs usually stay with their mother for about two and a half years.
- Even though they can be very big, brown bears can run really fast. Records show they can run at speeds of up to 30 miles per hour.

Lily's parents aren't the only ones who run a wildlife hospital.

Have you heard of Tiggywinkles – the world's busiest wildlife hospital? They take care of over 10,000 poorly animals every year and treat all kinds of wildlife, including hedgehogs, badgers, birds, foxes and deer.

If you are worried about a wild animal, you can have a look at their website for hints and tips about what to do.

www.tiggywinkles.com

Orchard Books supports Tiggywinkles.